Beth and the Bugs

Level 2D

Written by Sam Hay
Illustrated by Ann Johns

Ticktock

What is synthetic phonics?

Synthetic phonics teaches children to recognise the sounds of letters and to blend 'synthesise' them together to make whole words.

Understanding sound/letter relationships gives children the confidence and ability to read unfamiliar words, without having to rely on memory or guesswork; this helps them progress towards independent reading.

Did you know? Spoken English uses more than 40 speech sounds. Each sound is called a *phoneme*. Some phonemes relate to a single letter (d-o-g) and others to combinations of letters (sh-ar-p). When a phoneme is written down it is called a *grapheme*. Teaching these sounds, matching them to their written form and sounding out words for reading is the basis of synthetic phonics.

Consultant

I love reading phonics has been created in consultation with language expert Abigail Steel. She has a background in teaching and teacher training and is a respected expert in the field of Synthetic Phonics. Abigail Steel is a regular contributor to educational publications. Her international education consultancy supports parents and teachers in the promotion of literacy skills.

Reading tips

This book focuses on the th sound as in thing.

Tricky words in this book

Any words in bold do not sound exactly as they look (don't fit the usual sound-letter rules) or are new and have not yet been introduced.

Tricky words in this book:

the   I   said   my   her

Extra ways to have fun with this book

After the reader has finished the story, ask them questions about what they have just read:

What bugs does Beth find in her lunchbox?
What did Beth spot in the mud?

Explain that the two letters 'th' make one sound. Think of other words that use the 'th' sound, such as *thanks* and *think*.

I have lots of brothers and sisters and we all like to read stories about bugs!

A pronunciation guide

This grid highlights the sounds used in the story and offers a guide on how to say them.

s	a	t	p	i
as in sat	as in ant	as in tin	as in pig	as in ink
n	c	e	h	r
as in net	as in cat	as in egg	as in hen	as in rat
m	d	g	o	u
as in mug	as in dog	as in get	as in ox	as in up
l	f	b	j	v
as in log	as in fan	as in bag	as in jug	as in van
w	z	y	k	qu
as in wet	as in zip	as in yet	as in kit	as in quick
x	ff	ll	ss	zz
as in box	as in off	as in ball	as in kiss	as in buzz
ck	pp	nn	rr	gg
as in duck	as in puppy	as in bunny	as in arrow	as in egg
dd	bb	tt	sh	ch
as in daddy	as in chubby	as in attic	as in shop	as in chip
th	th			
as in them	as in thin			

Be careful not to add an 'uh' sound to 's', 't', 'p', 'c', 'h', 'r', 'm', 'd', 'g', 'l', 'f' and 'b'. For example, say 'fff' not 'fuh' and 'sss' not 'suh'.

Beth is on a bug trip with Miss Hill
and class 2.

Class 2 run up **the** path.

'**I** spot a thick slug in the mud!"
said Dot.

'I spot a red moth on that log!'
said Nat. 'I spot a thin bug!'
said Dom.

Beth is sad.
'I did not spot a bug,' said Beth.

'I cannot tick **my** bug list.'

'Picnic?' asks Miss Hill.

'Yum!' said Beth.
The kids sit on a big log.

Beth gets a bun from **her** bag.

But Beth has a shock!

'Bugs!' yells Beth.

Beth spots a lot of bugs in the bag.

Thud! The bag fell.
'Ants,' said Miss Hill.

'Top spot Beth!'

Beth can tick her bug list.

But Beth has lost her bun!

OVER **48** TITLES IN SIX LEVELS
Abigail Steel recommends...

Some titles from Level 1

I love reading phonics **Bad Rat**	I love reading phonics **The Best Gift**	I love reading phonics **Clint and Grant Play I-Spy**	I love reading phonics **Gran and Bret's Trip**
978-1-84898-600-8	978-1-84898-603-9	978-1-78325-098-1	978-1-78325-100-1

Other titles to enjoy from Level 2

I love reading phonics **Chuck and Duck**	I love reading phonics **Let's go to the Swings**	I love reading phonics **Kyle in Trouble**
978-1-84898-605-3	978-1-78325-102-5	978-1-78325-101-8

Some titles from Level 3

I love reading phonics **Bart's Go-Cart**	I love reading phonics **Queen Ella's Feet**	I love reading phonics **Puff Flies**	I love reading phonics **The Pop Duel**
978-1-78325-105-6	978-1-84898-609-1	978-1-84898-610-7	978-1-78325-108-7

An Hachette UK Company
www.hachette.co.uk

Copyright © Octopus Publishing Group Ltd 2012
First published in Great Britain in 2012 by TickTock, an imprint of Octopus Publishing Group Ltd,
Endeavour House, 189 Shaftesbury Avenue, London WC2H 8JY.
www.octopusbooks.co.uk
www.ticktockbooks.co.uk

ISBN 978 1 84898 607 7

Printed and bound in China
10 9 8 7 6 5 4 3